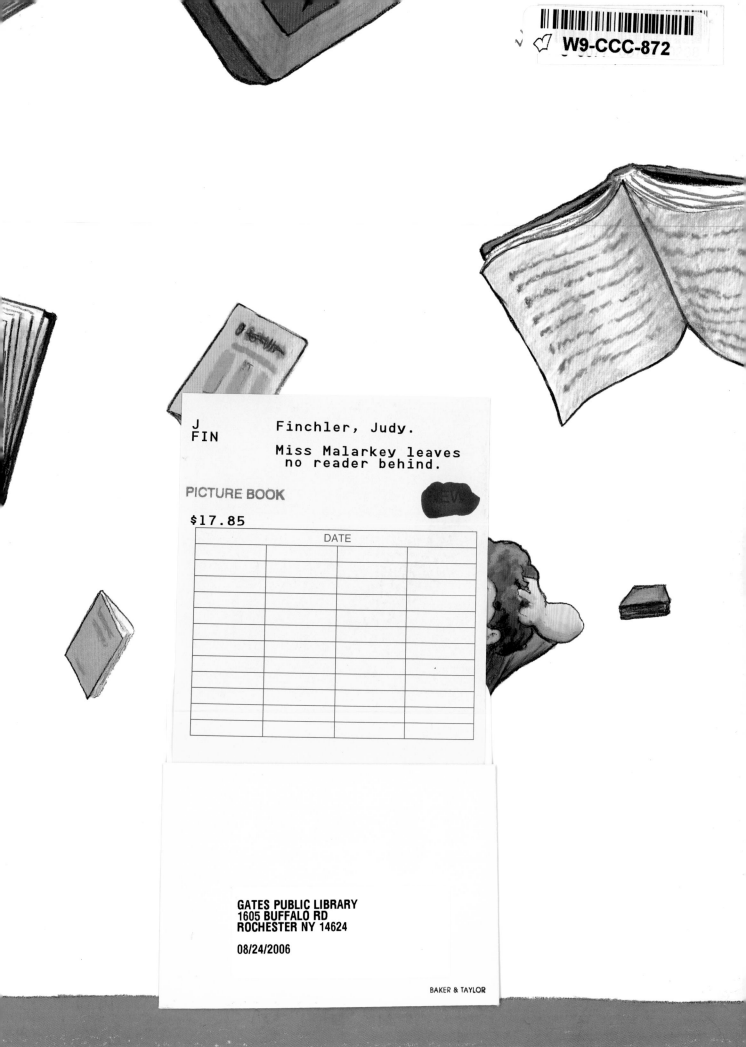

Miss Malarkey Leaves No Reader Behind

Judy Finchler & Kevin O'Malley

Illustrations by Kevin O'Malley

Walker & Company
New York

To my twin granddaughters,
Elana Harriet and Erica Sydney—
you are more beautiful and precious
than Grandma's jewels.
—J. F.

Text copyright © 2006 by Judy Finchler and Kevin O'Malley
Illustrations copyright © 2006 by Kevin O'Malley
All rights reserved. No part of this book may be reproduced or transmitted
in any form or by any means, electronic or mechanical, including photocopying,
recording, or by any information storage and retrieval system,
without permission in writing from the publisher.
First published in the United States of America in 2006 by
Walker Publishing Company, Inc.
Distributed to the trade by Holtzbrinck Publishers
For information about permission to reproduce selections from
this book, write to Permissions, Walker & Company,
104 Fifth Avenue, New York, New York 10011

Library of Congress Cataloging-in-Publication Data
Finchler, Judy.
Miss Malarkey leaves no reader behind / Judy Finchler and Kevin O'Malley;
illustrations by Kevin O'Malley.
p.   cm.
Summary: Miss Malarkey vows to find each of her students a book to love by the end
of the school year, but one video-game loving boy proves to be a challenge.
ISBN-10: 0-8027-8084-9 • ISBN-13: 978-0-8027-8084-3 (hardcover)
ISBN-10: 0-8027-8085-7 • ISBN-13: 978-0-8027-8085-0 (reinforced)
[1. Books and reading—Fiction. 2. Teachers—Fiction. 3. Schools—Fiction.]
I. O'Malley, Kevin, 1961–ill. II. Title.
PZ7.F495666Mll 2004   [Fic]—dc22   2005037182

The artist used markers and colored pencils to create the illustrations for this book.
Visit Walker & Company's Web site at www.walkeryoungreaders.com
Printed in China

2 4 6 8 10 9 7 5 3 1

All papers used by Walker & Company are natural, recyclable products
made from wood grown in well-managed forests. The manufacturing processes
conform to the environmental regulations of the country of origin.

It's the first week of school, and this year Miss Malarkey said our class would be doing the *Everybody Reads in America* program.

She thinks that reading is about the finest thing a person can do, and she promises to find each of us a book we'll love before the end of the year.

Our school is supposed to read 1,000 books by June 12.

Principal Wiggins says that if we can read that many books, he will dye his hair purple and sleep on the roof of the school. I'd love to see that, but there's one problem . . .

I hate reading.

In October, Miss Malarkey gave me a book of scary stories. I don't like scary stories.

I like video games, and so do my friends.

Adwin is from Senegal. He doesn't speak English very well yet, but he really likes math.

Sam is good at lacrosse.

Jamal likes to draw.

Me, I like aliens, race cars, funny jokes, chewing gum, hot sauce, and doing cannonballs at the pool.

Miss Malarkey handed out a
list of books that somebody
said we should try:

FIFTY NIFTY BOOKS FOR NOVEMBER:

Recommended reading list of the Montgomery County School Board and the
President's Council on Reading Advancement and Promotion Assessment

Fire! The Day Chicago Burned
Did a cow start the great Chicago fire of 1871?

Chad Shrub: Prince to President
A young boy overcomes wealth and privilege to become the leader of the free world.

Mary Sweetmary
A pretty pilgrim girl travels to the New World and discovers a whole new world—
of exciting outfits and hairstyles.

Who Knew You Could Do That with a Peanut?: The George Washington Carver Story
One man's obsession with a legume leads to many wonders.

Long-Dead Baseball Greats: Baseball in the 1890s
A look at the development of baseball and the famous names from long ago.

The Science of Food
Explore the science of why we eat and what we leave behind.

Melinda's Mother
Melinda is the only daughter of a famous actress. Will anyone ever notice her?

Now You Are a Man Now
...ar-old Ben Harbinger must grow up quickly when he becomes the capta...
...ddlewheel boat lost in a hurricane.

...del, Stop Playing with Your Food!
...An exploration of the life and times of genetics pioneer Gregor Mendel.

Why Mommy Cries
Life isn't easy for an American family forced to move to Paris.

The school year is going by fast.

It's already December. Everybody is reading. Everybody but me and my friends.

We walked by Suzy Curtsmirin. Her backpack was so crammed with books, she looked like she was gonna fall flat on her back.

"What's in the backpack?" I asked. "Rocks?"

We saw Larry Stork reading a book on his way home.
He walked right into a telephone pole.
Ellen Japson ran by really fast.
"Where's the fire?" yelled Sam.
"In the book I'm reading! It's great!" yelled Ellen.
"The world is going crazy," said Jamal.
We went to my house and played video games.

Every time we finish a book, Miss Malarkey puts a blue ribbon on the wall with our name and the book title.

She sure has put up a lot of ribbons.

Suzy Curtsmirin has twenty-five ribbons on the wall.

Charles Dewey has fifteen.

And Brenda Johns finished five books this week! I mean, FIVE BOOKS in ONE WEEK! How can she do that? Doesn't she eat?

Elastic Book Festival January 21st

Miss Malarkey keeps giving me books. She says she'll find a book for me if it kills her. I don't want her to die, so I told her I'd keep trying. When I tried to read one of them after I played video games, I fell asleep.

It's February now, and Miss Malarkey is still trying to find a book I'll love.

She gave me a fantasy book, but the names were confusing.

In March, Miss Malarkey gave me a book of jokes, but I'd heard them all before.

In April, she tried a book of poems . . . I don't know what she was thinking.

Miss Malarkey doesn't give up easily.

The fairies never dance by day,
for night is best—they think.
The fireflies turn on and off—
Twink! Blinkety! Wink!

Ugh!

In May, she gave me a book about crazy mixed-up explorer guys, but I lost interest before they even set sail.

It's June now, and my friends came over to play video games—everyone but Sam.

"Miss Malarkey give him a book Friday," said Adwin. "Maybe he reading?"

"No way," I said. "He's out playing some sport."

We called Sam's house.

His mother said, "He's busy right now. I'll have him call you when he's done. . . . He's reading."

It's been months since we started the *Oh Gee Wiz, Aren't Books Great* program.

Miss Malarkey keeps giving me books to read, but I just don't get it.

Our class has read 275 books. Our school has read 869 books. Adwin, James, and I have read zero.

Video games are just so much cooler.

Reading? I know how to read. But what's so great about books?

One day at lunch, I sat down with Sam, Adwin, and Jamal. Adwin kept looking down at his lap.

"Did you wet your pants or something?" I laughed.

"Not wet!" said Adwin, and he lifted up a book he was hiding under the table.

"Miss Malarkey give me this book. Good book about math guy. His name David Blackwell."

"That's great, Adwin," I said, "You enjoy your stupid book, but Jamal and I are going to be video game masters."

"Actually," said Jamal, "I thought that was a good book when I read it, too, and I don't think I even like math. I like when the guy said, 'I like pictures. Formulas and symbols—I don't especially like them.' He was a pretty cool guy."

My jaw hung open.
"How long have you
been reading books,
Jamal?"

"A while now, I guess. I didn't want to make you feel bad. See, Miss Malarkey gave me this book about a painter named Van Gogh. You know how I like cool pictures; this book had a lot of them."

My friends read now.

They still play video games, but not quite as much.

Sometimes, when they come over, they bring books and trade them.

Sometimes they barely even play the video games. They talk about books.

On June 10, our school had a big assembly for the reading program. We're getting close to the goal of reading 1,000 books. The teachers bought a special sleeping bag for Principal Wiggins for when he sleeps on the roof of the school.

The school has read 999 books. Our class has read 334.

The next day Miss Malarkey asked me to stay after school.

I thought maybe she was going to yell at me about all the books I didn't finish.

I tried to like reading books. I really did. I tried sports books, science books, joke books, fantasy, explorer, and detective books . . .

What was I supposed to do?

When I got to Miss Malarkey's room, she had this crazy smile on her face.

She said, "This year I found out a lot about you. I found out you don't like girl stories, dead baseball players, and math tricks. I found out you're not mean, you don't lie, and you love video games. You like cool sneakers, your lucky number is fifteen, and your favorite uncle is in the army. Your mother's name is Carol and your father's name is Bob.

"This year I found out even more about you. You, my boy, like aliens, race cars, funny jokes, chewing gum, hot sauce, and doing cannonballs at the pool."

Then she yelled . . .

I went home that day and started to read.
It was the greatest book ever made.
It had aliens and race cars and funny jokes and chewing gum
and hot sauce and cannonballs. It even had a pool!

I read right through dinner, and at ten o'clock my mom and dad came up to see if I was feeling all right.

The next day, Mom wrote a note to Miss Malarkey and told me to give it to her.

Hold on, I'm almost finished.

Turns out I hadn't read the 1,000th book; I read number 1,001.
That's okay because I got to read the greatest book ever.
Miss Malarkey gave me a hug and said, "Congratulations."

When school was over, everyone went outside and looked up to the roof.

We all yelled, "GOOD NIGHT, PRINCIPAL WIGGINS!"

Here are more great books for you to read (if you like the same things I do):

Aliens

Fat Men from Space by Daniel Manus Pinkwater, Random House, 1980.

Invaders from Outer Space by Dorling Kindersley, DK Readers, 1999.

Race Cars

The Race Car Alphabet by Brian Floca, Simon & Schuster, 2003.

NASCAR's Wildest Wrecks by Matt Doeden, Edge Books, 2005.

On the Track with Jeff Gordon by Matt Christopher, Little, Brown, 2001.

Jokes

Jokelopedia: The Biggest, Best, Silliest, Dumbest Joke Book Ever by Ilana Weitzman, Eva Blank, Roseanne Green, and Mike Wright, Workman, 2000.

The Everything Kids' Joke Book: Side-Splitting, Rib-Tickling Fun by Michael Dahl, Adams Media Corporation, 2002.

Chewing Gum, Hot Sauce, and Other Wacky Food Items

How Sweet It Is! (and Was): The History of Candy by Ruth Freeman Swain, Holiday House, 2003.

It's Disgusting and We Ate It: True Food Facts from Around the World and Throughout History by James Solheim, Simon & Schuster, 2001.

Swimming/Diving

Swimming and Diving by Christin Ditchfield, Children's Press, 2000.

Swimming and Diving: Olympic Library by John Verrier, Heinemann, 1996.

Here are some great books to help you find books about the things *you* love:

Valerie & Walter's Best Books for Children: A Lively, Opinionated Guide, Second Edition by Valerie L. Lewis and Walter M. Mayes, Quill, 2004.

100 Best Books for Children by Anita Silvey, Houghton Mifflin, 2004.

Great Books About Things Kids Love: More than 750 Recommended Books for Children 3 to 14 by Kathleen Odean, Ballantine, 2001.

The New York Times Parent's Guide to the Best Books for Children, Third Edition, by Eden Ross Lipson, Three Rivers Press, 2000.

How to Get Your Child to Love Reading: For Ravenous and Reluctant Readers Alike by Esme Raji Codell, Algonquin, 2003.

Best Books for Kids Who (Think They) Hate to Read: 125 Books That Will Turn Any Child into a Lifelong Reader by Laura Backes, Prima Lifestyles, 2001.

PLEASE SHARE YOUR THOUGHTS
ON THIS BOOK

comments:	comments:
comments:	comments:
comments:	comments:
comments:	comments:
comments:	comments:
comments:	comments: